For my Mum and Dad

– Nicola Edwards.

First published in the United Kingdom in 2002
by David Bennett Books Limited, an imprint of Chrysalis Books,
64 Brewery Road, London N7 9NT.

BRITISH LIBRARY CATALOGUING-IN-PUBLICATION DATA
A catalogue record for this book is available from the British Library.

ISBN 1 85602 433 4
Printed in Singapore by Imago

Goodnight Baxter

by Nicola Edwards

DAVID BENNETT BOOKS

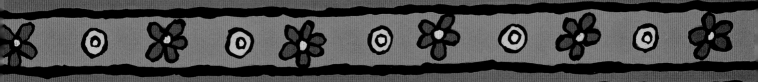

"Surprise!" said Daddy
as he opened his jacket
and out popped a puppy.

"I'm going to call him Baxter," said Charlie. Baxter licked Charlie's face.

Baxter and Charlie played all afternoon with the toys that Daddy had bought from the pet shop.

At bedtime, Charlie put
Baxter in his basket.

He gave Baxter
a goodnight kiss.
Then he went upstairs.

Baxter closed his eyes and tried to sleep...

in his basket...

on top of
his basket...

under his basket...

over the side
of his basket.

He even tried leaning
against his basket.
But it was no good.
He just couldn't sleep.

He had to go upstairs
and find Charlie.

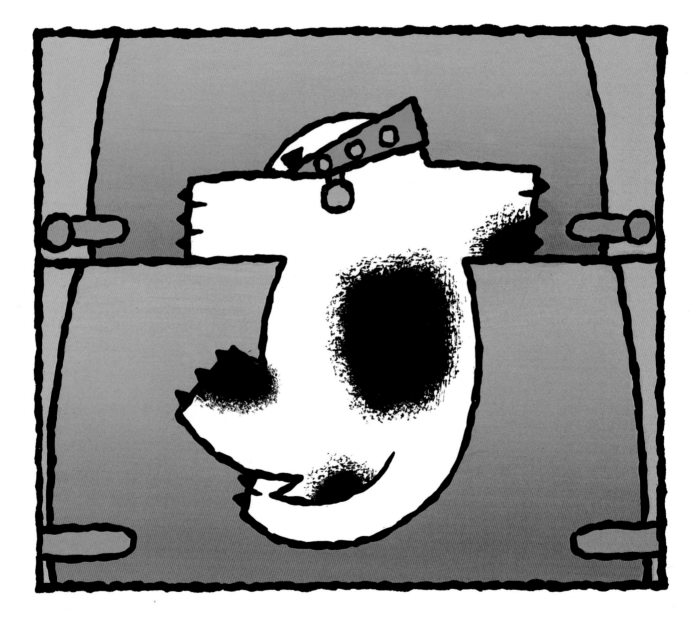

But every time Baxter
tried to climb the stairs

he tumbled back down.

So he sat at the bottom of the stairs and barked.

Charlie tiptoed quietly downstairs with a warm, cosy blanket for Baxter.

But Baxter kicked it off...

jumped out of his basket...

and barked for Charlie.

So Charlie carried his favourite teddy bear downstairs for Baxter

But Baxter tossed it away...

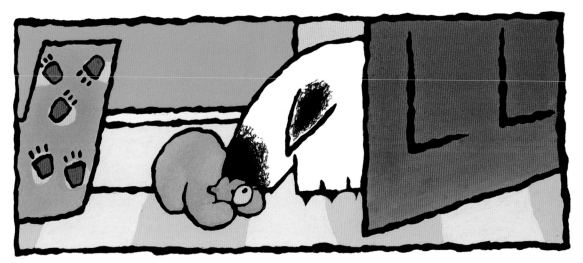

jumped out of his basket...

and barked and barked for Charlie.

Charlie even found his old dummy and took it downstairs for Baxter.

But Baxter spat it out...

jumped out of his basket...

and barked and barked and barked
for Charlie.

But this time Charlie
didn't wake up.
He was fast asleep.

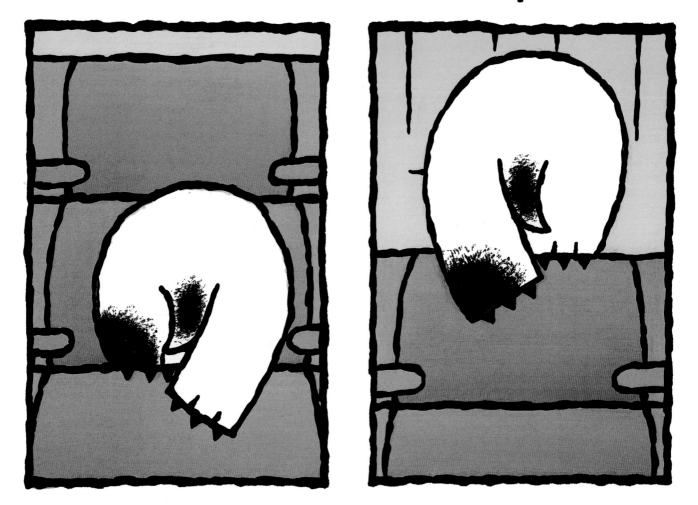

So Baxter wobbled and
stumbled up the stairs...
until he reached the top.

He pushed open Charlie's
door with his nose.

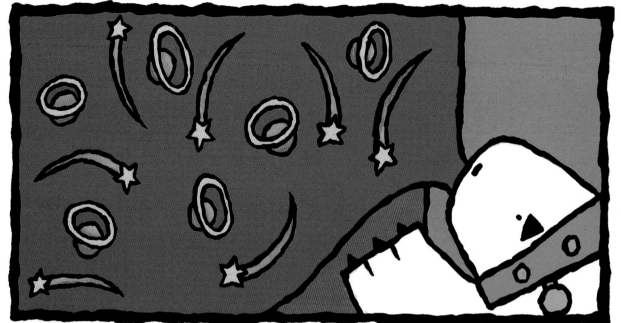

Baxter gave Charlie's
blanket a little tug...

he put his wet nose
on Charlie's hand...

he even licked one of
Charlie's ears... until
Charlie woke up.

Because **Baxter** didn't
want a blanket... or a
teddy   or a dummy

He wanted Charlie!

"Goodnight, Baxter!" said Charlie. And they both fell fast asleep.

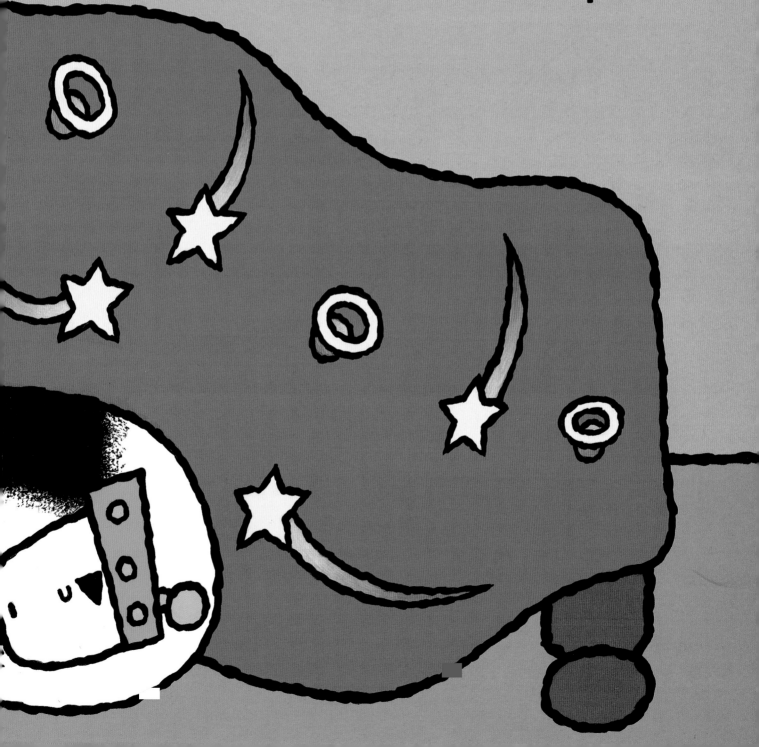